For Luke and James

High on the mountain

on a bluebird day,

the Gnarwhal is ready

for freshies to slay.

He straps on his board
as he sits on the ledge.
It's time to drop in
so he scoots to the edge.

He calls to his friends

"Come on guys, let's go!"

and the crew races down

to the valley below.

The Radypus skis
with breathtaking speed,
she dives down the slope
and is soon in the lead.

Zigging and zagging

with snow to her shin,

her face starts to show

a big powder grin!

She hears a loud noise

and turns back to see -

who is that coming

from out of the trees?

Jumping and turning
and end over end,
the Pow Cow is shredding
and going full send!

off jumps

ding on rails,

he catches an edge!

And suddenly bails...

His friends gather ro

concerned as can be

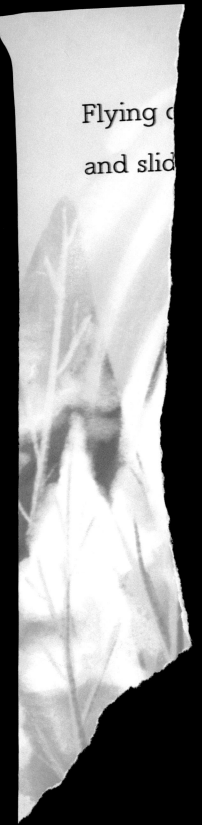

Flying

and slid

ound,

.

"Don't worry, I'm fine!

Let's go apres ski!"

Shreddy bear leads them
back home through the woods,
the winter wind blowing
snow down on their hoods.

Past rivers and meadows

the merry band roam,

then happily spot it –

that first glimpse of home.

Tucked under the pines,
it's Shreddy's retreat!
Now time to relax
and put up their feet.

Gnarwhal bakes cookies
and gives one to each,
while Radypus summons
the group for a speech.

"To a day full of
friendship, laughter, and fun!
Your sending and shredding
were second to none!"

They laugh by the fire,
each having their say,

and relive the glories
of their epic ski day.

The foursome grow tired
and soon go to sleep...

For dawn patrol beckons

with powder this deep...

The Adventure Friends will return...

Brian Duhon is a part-time adventurer
and first-time children's book author.
He lives in Boulder, Colorado with his wife
and two sons. He loves taking his boys up
into the mountains, and hopes this book
will inspire you to do the same.

Mousam Banerjee is a full time artist and
illustrator who loves to engage himself in
painting whimsical children's books to
realistic concept art. Born in an artistic family,
he was keen on creating original paintings
right from childhood. With a Post Graduate
Diploma in Fine Arts, he has now made a
career in digital illustrations. Please visit
www.illus-station.com